# I miss you, Grandad

www.tulipbooks.co.uk

This edition published by:

Tulip Books
Dept 302
43 Owston Road
Carcroft
Doncaster
DN6 8DA.

© Tulip Books 2013

First published in this edition by Evans Brothers Ltd, London in 2010.

Originally published in Belgium as *Opa duurt ontelbaar lang*
© 1995 Van In Publishers, Lier

British Library Cataloguing in Publication Data

Bode, Ann de.
  I miss you, grandad. -- (Side by Side)
  1. Grandfathers--Death--Juvenile fiction. 2. Grandparent and child--Juvenile fiction.
  3. Bereavement--Juvenile fiction. 4. Children's stories.
  I. Title II. Series
  839.3'1364-dc22

ISBN: 978-1-78388-004-1

Printed in Spain by Edelvives

Tom is rushing home after school. He wants to build a den in the garden.

'I'm home!' he cries.
'Hello everyone.'
But nobody says a word.

Why does everyone look so sad?
Why is Grandma crying?
Tom suddenly gets a strange
feeling in his stomach.

Mum gives Tom a big hug.
'Tom,' she says quietly. 'Something very
sad has happened. Grandad has died.'

Tom gives Grandma a big hug.
'Is Grandad dead for ever?' asks Tom.
'Yes,' says Grandma. 'When you die,
it's for ever.'

'Grandad made me a cup of tea this morning, just like he always does. But then he said he felt very tired, and went to lie down.

When I went to see him later,
I knew something was wrong.
He looked so peaceful, but
he had stopped breathing.'

No one quite knows what to do or say.
The time goes by slowly.

10

Dad comes home early.
He hugs Mum and she starts crying.
Tom's never seen his parents so upset before.

Then someone else rings the doorbell.
Tom's never seen him before.
'He's come to help us sort everything out,'
says Mum.

'He will help us to choose a
coffin for Grandad.'
'Will Grandad be scared?' asks Tom.
'No, when you're dead you don't feel
anything any more.'

'Come and help me choose some flowers for Grandad, Tom,' says Grandma. 'Beautiful flowers for the best grandad in the world,' says Tom.

Grandad's body is in the coffin. Everyone
is going to go and say goodbye to him.
'Will it be scary?' asks Tom.
'No, it's sad but it's not scary,' says Mum.
'It's as if Grandad is fast asleep.'

Mum shows Tom a picture
in the man's book.
'When Grandad is buried the coffin will
go in a car like this to the church.'
Good, thinks Tom. It's a special car for
a special grandad.

'Mum, where do people go when
they are dead?'
'If we keep thinking about him,' Mum
says, 'Grandad won't go anywhere.
He will stay with us in our hearts.'

Grandad used to know everything. But does
he know he's dead? thinks Tom suddenly.
Mum says, 'I don't think so. When you're
dead you don't know about anything any more.'

But Tom is worried, and he feels very sad.
What if Grandad doesn't know he's dead?
I must tell him! he thinks. But how?

'You're looking sad,' says Tom's neighbour.
'I need to tell Grandad something,' he says.
'Can't you find him?'
'No, he's died,' says Tom.

The neighbour comes to sit next to Tom.
'Sometimes when someone has died,
we say they have passed away, or
gone to the clouds.'
They both look up – no Grandad there.

Tom thinks – maybe Grandad has gone to a town called 'The Clouds'?
He goes to find the phonebook. He will try to ring Grandad there!

'I'm sorry, Tom,' says Dad.
'You can't ring Grandad.
But you can think about him very hard.
Why don't you look after his goldfish?
It will make you think of Grandad.'

That night, Tom can't sleep.
Being dead is very serious, he thinks.
He tries to imagine what it's like,
but he can't.

He looks at the picture of Grandad
next to his bed. Grandad is smiling.
He wouldn't be smiling if he knew
he was dead, Tom thinks.

Suddenly Tom has an idea! He'll write Grandad a letter, and put it in the coffin when they go to see him for the last time.

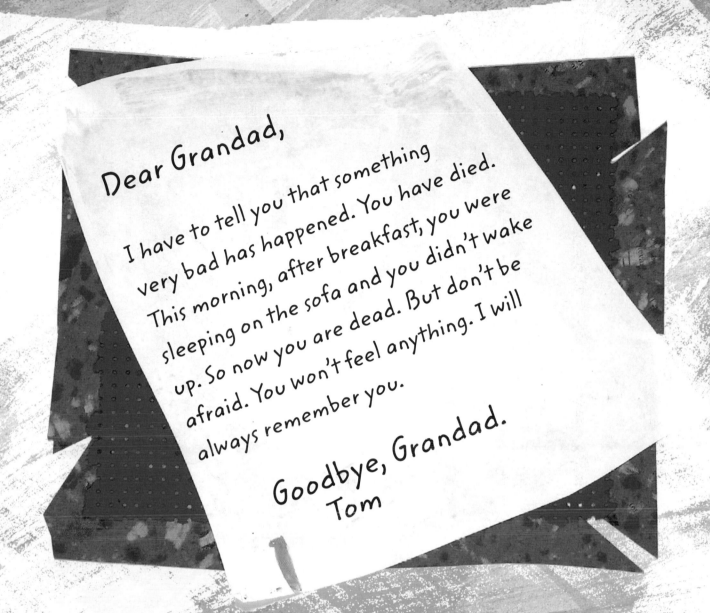

Dear Grandad,

I have to tell you that something very bad has happened. You have died. This morning, after breakfast, you were sleeping on the sofa and you didn't wake up. So now you are dead. But don't be afraid. You won't feel anything. I will always remember you.

Goodbye, Grandad.
Tom

Tom writes a letter telling Grandad that he has died. He tells him not to be afraid, and promises to remember him always. Tom feels better and finally goes to sleep.

He dreams that Grandad is
tapping at the window.
'Hello Tom,' says Grandad. Then he starts
to move away, getting fainter and fainter.

Tom tries to give him the letter.
He holds it out of the window.
Grandad is too far away, but Tom feels the
letter floating out into the night sky.

Then Tom feels a tap on
his shoulder. It's Dad.
'You've been sleepwalking, Tom.
Time to go back to bed.'

Back in bed, Tom sees that the letter has gone! It wasn't a dream! Now Grandad will be able to read it, he thinks.

Outside, the wind carries the letter higher and higher, up into the dark night, until all you can see is a small white dot, like a bird flying to its nest.